ROSE BLANCHE

ROSE BLANCHE
A RED FOX BOOK: 978 0 099 43950 9

First published in Great Britain by Jonathan Cape,
an imprint of Random House Children's Books

Jonathan Cape edition published 1985
Red Fox edition published 2004

5 7 9 10 8 6 4

Illustrations © 1985 Roberto Innocenti

First edition of Rose Blanche published by Creative Education, an imprint of The Creative Company, Mankato, Minnesota

Text of Jonathan Cape edition copyright © Ian McEwan, 1985

Red Fox Books are published by Random House Children's Books,
61-63 Uxbridge Road, London W5 5SA,
a division of The Random House Group Ltd.
Addresses for companies within The Random House Group Limited
can be found at: www.randomhouse.co.uk/offices.htm

THE RANDOM HOUSE GROUP Limited Reg. No. 954009
www.rbooks.co.uk
Printed in Italy

~ROSE BLANCHE~

ROBERTO INNOCENTI

TEXT BY IAN McEWAN
based on a story by Christophe Gallaz

RED FOX

When wars begin people often cheer. The sadness comes later. The men from the town went off to fight for Germany. Rose Blanche and her mother joined the crowds and waved them goodbye. A marching band played, everyone cheered, and the fat mayor made a boring speech.

There were jokes and songs and old men shouted advice to the young soldiers. Rose Blanche was shivering with excitement. But her mother said it was cold. Winter was coming.

Then there were lorries grinding through the narrow streets day and night, and lumbering tanks made sparks on the cobblestones. The noise was fantastic. The soldiers in the lorries sang songs. They smiled and winked at the children as if they were old friends. The children always waved back.

Rose Blanche often went shopping for her mother. There were long queues outside the shops, but no one grumbled. Everybody knew that food was needed for the soldiers who were always hungry.

Many things did not change at all. Rose Blanche still played with her friends. She did her homework after supper and went to school early in the morning with her lunch in her satchel.

And when school was over, she walked her favourite way home, along the river. At home her mother was always waiting for her with a hot drink.

Nobody knew where all the lorries were going. But people in the town talked about them. Some said they were going to a place just outside the town.

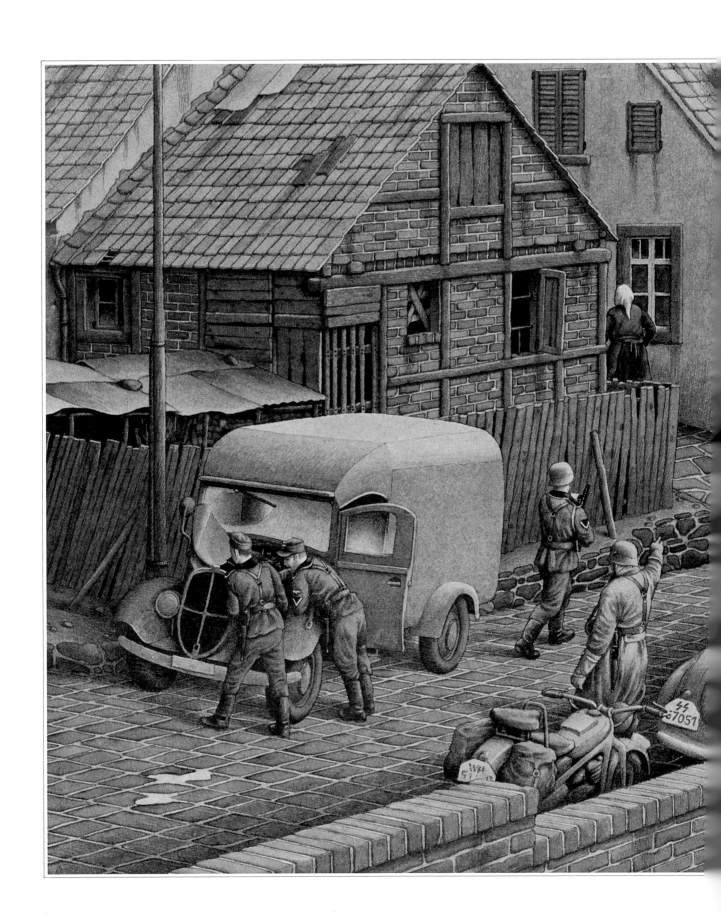

One day a lorry broke down. Rose Blanche saw two soldiers trying to repair the engine. Suddenly a little boy leapt from the back of the lorry and ran down the street.

A soldier shouted, Stop or I'll shoot.

The boy ran straight into the arms of the fat mayor.

The mayor was immensely pleased with himself. He dragged the boy by the scruff of the neck back to the lorry.

One of the soldiers was furious and shouted at the boy who burst into tears.

The boy was thrown back into the lorry. Rose Blanche saw other pale faces in the gloom, when the door banged shut and the lorry drove away in a cloud of diesel fumes.

Rose Blanche was furious at the way they had treated the little boy. Where were they taking him? She followed the lorry right through the town. She was a fast runner; she knew all the short-cuts. Winding streets forced the lorry to go slowly.

She ran along rutted tracks, across fields, over ditches and frozen puddles. She climbed under fences and barriers in places she wasn't meant to go.

Rose Blanche took a short-cut through the forest where bare
branches scratched her face. The road was below her, the lorry
was a long way ahead. She was so tired, she felt like giving up.
   Then she stumbled into a clearing and could hardly believe
what she saw.

Dozens of silent, motionless children stared at her from behind a barbed wire fence. They hardly seemed to breathe.

Their eyes were large and full of sorrow. They stood like ghosts, watching as she came close. One of them called for food, and others took up the cry.

Food, food, please be our friend. Please give us something to eat, little girl.

But she had nothing to give them, nothing at all. The cries died down, the silence returned. The winter sun was setting, the chilly wind made the barbed wire moan. Rose Blanche turned for home. Their sad and hungry eyes followed her into the forest.

Rose Blanche told no one, not even her mother, what she had seen. All through the bitter winter she took extra food to school, jam and apples from the cellar. And yet she was growing thinner all the time. At home she secretly saved the food off her own plate.

In the town people were no longer patient when they waited in the queues. No one had enough to eat except the mayor who was as fat as ever.

Rose Blanche slipped away from school as early as she could and, clasping her heavy bag, headed towards the forest.

The children were always waiting for her by the fence. When they took the food, careful not to touch the electric wires, their thin hands trembled.

Rose Blanche learned their names, told them hers and told them all about her school.

The children said little in reply. Huddled together, they stared through the fence into the distance.

Even at night Rose Blanche made her journey to the forest.
The snow was melting now and the track was muddy.

Others travelling under the cover of dark – soldiers, thousands of them, exhausted, wounded, dispirited – poured back through the town and on into the night. There was no singing or waving now.

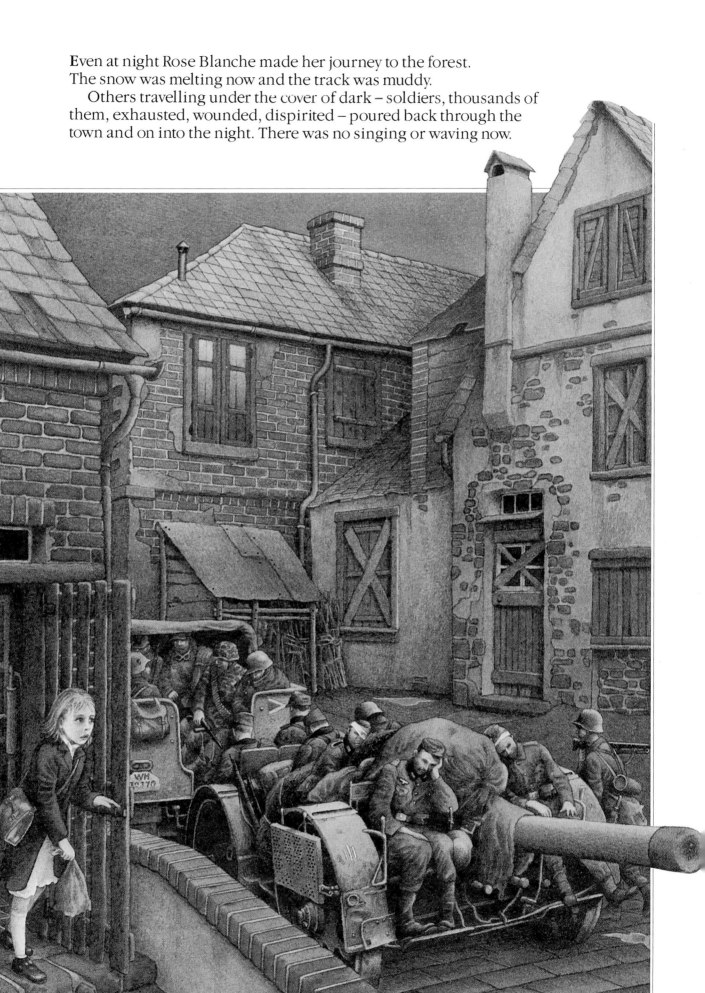

Then one morning the whole town decided to leave. People were frightened. They carried bags, and furniture and pets, they loaded wheelbarrows and carts. The mayor was one of the first to leave. He had taken off the bright armband he had once been so proud of.

That was the day Rose Blanche disappeared. Her mother
searched frantically for her all over the emptying town. She asked
everyone she met if they had seen her daughter.
    She's probably with friends, ahead, they told her. Don't worry.
Pack your bags and come with us.

Thick fog shrouded the forest and it was hard to find the way. Rose's feet were muddy and frozen. Her clothes were torn, and at last she arrived at her usual place.

She stood by the clearing as though in a dream. Everything was so different it was hard to think clearly.

Behind her were figures moving through the fog. Tired and fearful soldiers saw danger everywhere.

   As Rose Blanche turned to walk away, there was a shot, a sharp and terrible sound which echoed against the bare trees.

Meanwhile there were different soldiers passing through the little town. Their language was strange, their uniform unfamiliar, and though they were tired, they were cheerful. The war was almost over.

Rose Blanche's mother never found her little girl.
As the weeks went by another, gentler invasion began.

The cold retreated, fresh grasses advanced across the land.
There were explosions of colour. Trees put on their bright new
uniforms and paraded in the sun. Birds took up their positions
and sang their simple message.

Spring had triumphed.